D1249701

Presented to

_____

From

_____

Date

_____

The Incredible Discovery of Lindsey Renee

Illustrated by Irena Roman

Joni Eareckson Tada

CROSSWAY BOOKS · WHEATON, ILLINOIS

A DIVISION OF GOOD NEWS PUBLISHERS

PUBLISHER'S ACKNOWLEDGMENT

The publisher wishes to acknowledge that the text for *The Incredible
Discovery of Lindsey Renee* appeared originally as "It's in God's Hands" in
Tell Me the Truth, copyright 1997, written by Joni Eareckson Tada and
Steve Jensen and illustrated by Ron DiCianni. Special thanks to Ron DiCianni
for the idea and vision behind the creation of the series. More stories in the
"Tell Me" series—*Tell Me the Story, Tell Me the Secrets, Tell Me the Promises,
Tell Me Why*, all published by Crossway Books—are available at your local bookstore.

The Incredible Discovery of Lindsey Renee
Text copyright © 2001 by Joni Eareckson Tada
Illustrations copyright © 2001 by Irena Roman
Published by Crossway Books
a division of Good News Publishers
1300 Crescent Street
Wheaton, Illinois 60187

All rights reserved.
No part of this publication may be reproduced, stored in
a retrieval system or transmitted in any form by any means, electronic,
mechanical, photocopy, recording, or otherwise, without the prior permission
of the publisher, except as provided by USA copyright law.

Book design by Uttley/DouPonce DesignWorks
First printing 2001
Printed in USA
ISBN 1-58134-195-4

LIBRARY OF CONGRESS CATALOGING-IN-PUBLICATION DATA

Tada, Joni Eareckson.
The incredible discovery of Lindsey Renee/text by Joni Eareckson Tada; illustrated by Irena Roman.
p. cm.
Appeared originally as "It's in God's Hands" in *Tell Me the Truth* © 1997.
Summary; A mysterious man helps Lindsey make the right choice when she has to decide between
putting her money in the missions offering at church or using it to buy a new sweater at the mall.
ISBN 1-58134-195-4
[1. Christian life—Fiction.] i. Roman, Irena, ill. II. Title.
PZ7.T116 in 2000
[E]--dc21   00-009403
                                   CIP

10   09   08   07   06   05   04   03   02   01
15 14 13 12 11 10 9 8 7 6 5 4 3 2 1

To the *real* Lindsey Renee
and her sisters,
Rachel Leann and Eva Marie

Lindsey squirmed against the end of the church pew, trying her best to find a comfortable position. She had sat with her family on this exact bench hundreds of times, but it never felt so hard as it did tonight. Maybe it was because it was a Saturday night missions conference, and she knew she'd be back in the same pew early the next morning. Maybe it was because she didn't like stories about crocodiles, mosquitoes, and snakes. But thirteen-year-old Lindsey had another reason. She was dying to be at the mall with her friends.

"Lindsey Renee," her mother leaned over and whispered, "straighten up."

She huffed and did as she was told. But inside she was still slouching.

After the last missionary speaker left the pulpit, the pianist played a hymn, and Pastor Martin stepped up to make an announcement. "Friends, we've heard some marvelous testimonies this evening from our missionaries on the field. They've sacrificed a great deal to serve God in these foreign countries, and I want us to consider giving a special offering as the plate is passed tonight. Let's pray!"

Lindsey bowed her head and tried her best to pray. She felt guilty she hadn't paid attention to the speakers. She felt guilty that her mind kept wandering to the mall. But she really squirmed when the ushers began passing the plates. Reaching into her pocket, she clutched a five-dollar bill. It was the part of her monthly allowance she had promised her folks she'd give to the missions conference. Lindsey sighed. She would really rather put the five dollars toward the cute sweater she had seen at The Gap.

The ushers drew closer. Lindsey squirmed more. Suddenly she cupped her hand and hurriedly whispered to her mother, "I've got to go to the bathroom!" Without really getting permission, she jumped up and escaped out the side door right before the offering plate reached her row.

"Whew! Just in the nick of time!" she said quietly as she shut the door behind her and leaned against it. From there she walked down the dark hallway to the rest room. She entered, unfolded the bill, and held it up to the mirror. Happy thoughts of a new sweater mixed with feelings of guilt. Lindsey stuffed the bill back into her pocket and decided she'd better get back to the service. The offering plate had surely passed her row by now.

As she was heading up the dark hallway, Lindsey noticed a strange and very bright light streaming from a half-opened door. She peered around it and spied an older man, with a head of wild white hair and horn-rimmed glasses, hunched over a computer. He wore suspenders, a white shirt with sleeves rolled up, and a tweed vest. His jacket hung on the back of the chair, and several high stacks of thick books were piled on the table. He was typing fast and furiously. Lindsey had never seen anybody the age of her grandparents look so at home with a computer.

"Please do come in, Lindsey Renee," he said without looking up. Lindsey wrinkled her forehead, wondering how he knew her name.

"I'm Mr. Billingsley, and I've been expecting you," he turned and said with a smile.

"Weird," Lindsey murmured, but something about his funny hair and kind smile put her at ease, as though she knew him from the Discovery channel or had seen him in her science book. Lindsey walked slowly into the room and asked, "What are you working on?" like they were old friends.

"Why, this is your Book of Life," he said, patting the nearest stack of books.

This isn't weird; this is way out! she thought, feeling as though she had stepped into one of those silly skits they do at vacation Bible school.

Mr. Billingsley smiled and shook his finger. "I can tell you don't believe me, Lindsey Renee. And so, here—" He cracked open one of the books, thumbed through a few pages, straightened his glasses, and read: "'Date, April 23, 1992. Scene, the lunch table in the elementary school cafeteria. It is Alexandra Kerr's first day at school since moving to the neighborhood. Lindsey Renee Schroeder asks Alexandra to sit with her. Makes big impression on Alexandra, who happens to notice Lindsey's cross around her neck.'"

Lindsey's mouth dropped open. "How do you know about that?" she asked, disbelieving. "That was six years ago when I was in third grade!"

"Yes, and after her parents moved again two years later, little Alex remembered your thoughtfulness. She also remembered that cross, and so when she was invited to Sunday school, she went. What's more, Alex accepted the Lord Jesus as her Savior. You played a part in that," Mr. Billingsley said warmly.

Lindsey shook her head, as if to wake herself from a dream. She drew closer to the book, placed her hand on it, and decided to test this strange but very nice man at his odd game. She told him about the time she lost her Bible at camp last summer. "What happened to it?" she challenged.

Mr. Billingsley reached for a different book in the pile (explaining that her Book of Life was written in many volumes), flipped it open, and pointed Lindsey to the section that explained the Bible's whereabouts. She read the paragraph, mumbling, "'After camp ended, a kid from another church found it under Lindsey Renee's bunk. He saw all the neat things she had underlined in her Bible . . . made him want to get closer to God.' Wow!" she said, looking up. "I remember being so upset that I lost it and that God didn't answer my prayer to find it! This is neat!"

"Now," Mr. Billingsley said, pulling up his chair, "let's get down to business. Would you be in agreement with God as to how He plans for this evening's events to turn out? You do have a say in it, you know."

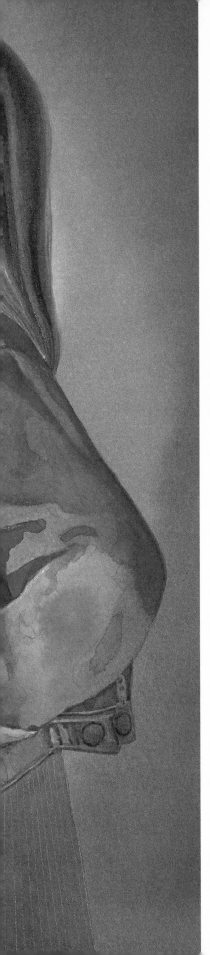

"I do?" Lindsey asked, puzzled.

"Oh, yes," he said, his hands waiting on the computer keys. "I don't have time to teach a course in God's control and your free will, but you have been, as it says in the Bible, chosen to be one of God's people. And God 'makes everything agree with what he decides and wants.' It's your choice, Lindsey Renee, but God's plan."

This was all too hard for a thirteen-year-old to understand, but Lindsey wasn't about to argue with the Bible or Mr. Billingsley. "So what am I supposed to choose?"

"What you intend to do about Pastor Martin's sermon tonight, of course."

Lindsey had entirely forgotten about his challenge to give money to the missionaries.

She fingered the crumpled bill in her pocket. She thought about the offering—and then the sweater. Which would it be? Stalling for time, she asked, "First, can I know how it's all going to turn out?"

"Ho, ho, my dear," Mr. Billingsley chided her, "this isn't Psychic Hot Line. You are the only one who can choose. But I can show you this." He looked up something, turned to his computer, typed quickly, and then punched the "enter" key. Immediately, on the screen appeared the image of a man on the edge of a jungle. It looked hot, and he looked upset. His hands were black with grease. He was holding a wrench and leaning over the open engine hood of a small airplane. Words kept flashing on the bottom of the screen: "Jim Singleton. Missionary pilot. Has prayed for help. Awaiting God's answer."

Lindsey leaned closer to the screen. The jungle pilot was shaking his head, as if he couldn't fix the engine.

"What's this got to do with tonight?" Lindsey asked.

Mr. Billingsley typed in more commands, but the computer kept flashing, "Security Password Required." He leaned back and sighed, "I don't have clearance for the answer to your question. But you definitely have something to do with this pilot. Exactly what, I cannot say." He shook his head and then punched a few keys. Another file popped up on the screen. Mr. Billingsley adjusted his glasses and read the words on the screen. "I can tell here that Jim Singleton desperately needs a high-performance spark plug. The kind that tropical heat and rain won't hurt. Apparently, though, those things are pretty expensive." He then turned to Lindsey. "And, as you heard tonight's speakers say, missionaries aren't rich."

Lindsey clutched the five-dollar bill. "Mr. Billingsley," she said as she began backing away, "can you stay right here? Don't move; don't go anywhere. I've got something to do, and I'll be right back!" She bolted out the door and down the hallway. She slipped through the side door and slid into her pew, scanning the sanctuary. Lindsey's shoulders slumped. She let out a groan. The offering was over, and the plates and ushers were nowhere to be seen.

Her mother noticed the groan. "What's going on?" she asked. "Are you ill?"

"Mom," Lindsey asked urgently, "how much does an airplane spark plug cost?"

Her mother gave her a strange look, thinking for sure a fever had hit her daughter. The service ended, and Lindsey and her family stood to leave. As everyone gathered coats and Bibles, Lindsey made a fast escape to go see Mr. Billingsley. She had to explain that she wanted—she really wanted—to help the jungle pilot, but it was too late.

She darted through the hall to the room and then screeched to a halt. Gone was the computer and the books. And sitting in Mr. Billingsley's chair was an elder who, along with several others, was counting the evening offering. "Oh, great," Lindsey shouted, "I'm not too late!"

"Lindsey, what's up?" Mr. Johnson asked.

"I want to buy a spark plug. Mr. Billingsley said it was needed right away," she insisted, unfolding the bill and placing it squarely on the table.

"Huh?" He gave her a puzzled look.

"And it's to go directly to help the pilot. Okay?" she pleaded, backing away toward the door. "Can you do that? Please!"

"Okay, okay." Mr. Johnson smiled, as though to quiet her down. He reached for the money on the table and gently placed it in the offering plate. "We promise we'll do it—right, gentlemen?" He glanced at the others. They nodded.

Lindsey thanked them all and hurried out of the room.

"Who's Mr. Billingsley?" asked Mr. Johnson as he took his pen and marked the amount in his ledger.

At that instant, as his pen wrote "$5," a clerk in a warehouse thousands of miles away received a phone call, checked his list, and made a few notes on his clipboard. His boss signed the forms and yelled to the ground crew at the airport, "Okay, men, load that box that's been waiting. Orders just came down from headquarters. Hurry. The plane's ready to taxi out!"

The ground crew rushed to an airplane waiting on the runway, ready to take off for the jungles of Brazil. They hoisted the box into the open cargo door. The side of the box read: "Handle with Care. High-Performance Spark Plugs."

And at that instant, a pilot leaned on his engine hood to take a break from his work. As he did, he heard the scratchy sound of his air base calling over the radio, "Jim Singleton, come in. We've got those spark plugs coming your way."

The pilot wiped his brow and smiled. *God,* he thought, *is so good. And always in control.*

At that moment, half a world away, a thirteen-year-old, still wondering if she had had a dream, smiled and thought the same. *God is good.* Then she shoved her hands into her empty pockets. *Yes, He is very, very good.*